MW00892023

Copyright © 2019 Pequid Publishing
Story © David Bolton
Cover, design and illustration © Ute Simon
David Bolton, (415) 286-1294, dmbolton567@gmail.com
Ute Simon, (323) 632-2291, ute@illustratrix.com

Nimby, Orell & the Pequids Egg

by David Bolton
Illustrated by Ute Simon

2/2/20

1

The Finding

To Dolores Mendieta
Thank you for reading

Nimby laid on his back, arms folded behind his head. As he rested on a log, he gazed up at the drifting clouds and sighed, "Wow, that was incredible."

"It sure was," answered Orell, as he blew on a dandelion, setting free its blossoms. He watched them float away, and turned to Nimby. "I want to do it again".

"Me too." murmured Nimby.

Orell sat down next to Nimby in the warm afternoon sun and they both closed their eyes remembering.

Nimby tiptoed as quietly as possible through the vacant lot, careful not to step on any dry twigs. He knew if he could just be quiet long enough Orell would give up his position.

The brothers were playing their favorite game, 'Hide and Bleat'. Nimby stopped, closed his eyes and sniffed the air. He smelled something sweet, and fruity. He knew he was close now and the closer he got to an old plank of wood leaning against the fence, the stronger the scent became.

He moved toward the plank and threw it aside. Underneath it on a piece of paper was a cherry lollipop.

"Bah", yelped Orell, leaping out from behind a bush and bounded for the Tag Tree. He tagged it with his right fore foot. "I win! I win!"

"Yes," replied Nimby. "You do. But so do I."

Nimby slowly lifted the sucker to his lapping tongue and purred as he closed his lips around it.

"That's mine, that's mine," shouted Orell running toward Nimby.

Nimby kept turning away as Orell tried to get the sucker from him.

"Come on Nim, it's mine."

Nimby laughed. "Tastes like it's mine now. Part of the cost of winning, I'd say. Bahhhh!"

Orell stopped trying to get it back, sat on his haunches, and wailed. "Aaahhh".

"Ok, ok. Don't cry about it. I was just playing. Here, take it back." Orell reached for the sucker and just as he almost touched it, Nimby pulled it back.

"Ha ha," Nimby laughed, biting off a piece of the sucker. "Just kidding."

Orell wailed and began to cry. Nimby handed what was left of the sucker to Orell and smiled.

"Yum, this is really good. You don't have any germs do you?" asked Nimby, slurping on the candy. "Not that it matters."

Orell didn't answer. He was busy devouring what was left of the sucker and poking around the base of a tree.

Nimby moved over to see what was so interesting.

There, half covered in a clump of grass was the largest egg he'd ever seen. It was of a light green color with dark brown rumpled veins running about it's outside.

"Wow", exclaimed Nimby reaching for the egg.

Orell grabbed his arm. "No, no. Don't touch it, Nimby. Mom says if you touch an egg, its parents won't want it anymore."

Nimby slowly moved his hoof toward the egg while keeping an eye on Orell.

"Don't do it, Nimby."

Nimby smiled. "I'm not", but kept reaching toward the egg. As he was just about to touch the egg, Orell butted him away. Nimby staggered back a couple of steps then butted Orell sending him sprawling.

"I wasn't going to touch it. I was only playing."

The boys looked up into the tree, but there was no nest. There were a half a dozen or so small birds, so Nimby shouted, "Is this your egg?" The birds looked down at the boys, chirped and flew off.

"I don't think that was their egg."

"Me neither, it's bigger than all of them put together." "The boys looked all over the lot but there was no nest.

"I wonder where it came from?"

"I wonder what's in it?"

"Maybe it's a lizard...or a snake."

The kids backed away from the egg.

"Well, what should we do?"

"Let's go ask mom!"

The boys bolted from the lot, and up the trail to their home.

Mom watched the boys from the kitchen window as they crawled under the gated fence and ran up to the front door shouting, "Mom, mom, guess what?

Before they could get through the door she halted them.

"Hold it right there children. Have you wiped your hooves?"

The kids looked down at their muddy, grassy hooves then up to their mom.

"No. Not exactly."

Mom folded her arms as the boys stepped down from the stoop and onto a mat. They picked up a brush and rag and began cleaning.

"Mom, we found an egg in the old vacant lot and, and it's big, and green, and..."

"Yeah, mom, and it's got brown veins on it!"

The boys continued cleaning their hooves and brushing their coats as they finished their story.

"There's only one thing to do," said mom. "You must go to Malik and seek his guidance."

"Malik", they chorused, "You mean Malik, the...?"

"That's right."

"By ourselves?"

"That's right."

"Are you sure," asked Orell. "Just me and Nimby?"

"Excuse me," answered their mom, giving him a stern look.

"I mean, Nimby and I."

The astonished brothers could hardly believe their ears.

"I remember," said their mother, "when Malik stood up to a knasher."

"A knasher," asked the boys in awe?

"That's right."

The boys sat on their haunches and listened wide-eyed with mouths ajar as their mother continued the story.

"When I was just about your age, a knasher found our village. Goodness, it was just awful. Several kids just disappeared. Everyone looked high and low for them, and then they found...

... oh, it's just too horrible to say. Afterwards, no one dared stray far from his or her home. That's when Malik came to the center of the town and told everyone to stay inside, that he was going to summon the knasher and deal with it once and for all. He opened a bag of something that smelled like, something rotting and just stood there waiting. Then in the distance I heard a great roar, the roar of a knasher. And believe you me, I was scared to the bone.

The roars continued and got louder as it came into town. The beast snarled and whipped its tail as it approached Malik, but he stood fast. It began to circle him, making ready to pounce. That's when he reached into his pouch and blew something into the knashers face, and the queerest thing happened."

Right at that moment, Nimby slyly poked Orell on his rump and growled; sending him leaping into his mother's arms with a yelp.

"Mom! Nimby scared me!"

"Nimby, don't scare your brother. You wouldn't like it if he scared you."

"Yes, I would."

"Nimby?"

"Sorry mom. Sorry Orell."

Mom gave Orell a hug and a kiss and released him as he leapt to the floor.

Orell sat back down on his brother's side forcing him to scoot over.

Their mother didn't notice and seemed to be lost in thought for a moment before she spoke.

"Yes, if anyone can help you, it would be Malik. That's who you've got to see." Mom turned, smiling to herself and went back to her chores.

"Mom," cried Nimby, "what happened?"

"Oh, right, where was I?

"He blew something in the knashers face," gasped Orell.

"Right. You wouldn't believe it, but that mean old knasher began rolling around on the ground and rubbing its face in the dirt and leaping in the air. Then it started running as fast as it could towards absolutely nothing. It just kept running and leaping in different directions like it had lost its mind. Then it ran out of town and Malik said he would plant seeds to grow bushes of the stuff he blew on the knasher throughout the kingdom, and that's the last we ever saw of that mean old knasher, or any other!"

The boys were speechless.

"Well, what are you waiting for, a written invitation? Go see Malik."

With that the kids took a deep breath and bounded off toward the gate.

"Orell, Nimby", called their mother, "the gate was not put there to crawl under."

"Yes, mom," they answered running to the gate and leaping over it.

Mom laughed to herself as her offspring bounded down the hill, "My boys".

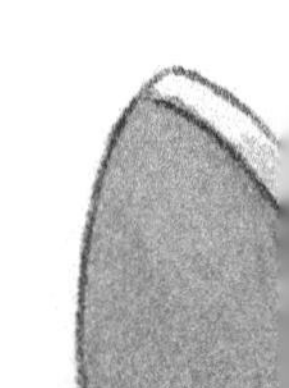

Malik's home was set upon the highest point in the countryside just above the village. Of course, where else would it be? The house was more like a castle, several stories tall with dozens of windows on each floor. Like a jewel struck by light, the windows sent reflected sunbeams about the village and the valley beneath.

Now, the kids had run most of the way but as they approached the building they were overwhelmed by its height. As they turned the last bend on the trail they stopped in their tracks, speechless. Though they'd seen the structure from a distance, they'd never actually been so close.

The building loomed over them. They slowly stepped forward, their heads tilted back as far as they could but still could not see the top of the house. Time seemed to stop when they reached the edge of it's bordering white picket fence, mouths ajar, imagining what wonders were within.

"Well, are you just going to stand there gawking?" asked a voice at their knees.

The boys leaped back from the fence with a shriek. They hadn't noticed the gardener rooting around near their hooves.

"Oh, he, he." they laughed. "Hi, we're looking for Malik, the...

"I know. I know." said the gardener. "Well, it seems you've come to the right place."

The gardener pulled a couple of enormous tomatoes from a vine and offered them to the boys, who gratefully accepted.

The boys began munching on the fruit and the gardener continued with his work, talking to his herbs and vegetables as he poked at their roots with a hoof spade. "That's it, my little babies. We're going to do wonderful things together, aren't we?"

Nimby whispered into Orells ear. "I think he might have dug up one too many worms."

"And what," asked the gardener, "may I ask do you want of Malik, to find out just what number of worms is too many?"

The gardener, in a long moment of silence, dubiously eyed them.

Nimby lowered his head and mumbled, "Sorry sir. That's not why we're here."

Orell cleared his throat and spoke. "Well, actually, we found something."

"Umph." grunted the gardener.

Between mouthfuls of tomato, the boys retold their story leaving out no detail, of playing Hide and Bleat, finding the egg, telling their mom, leaping over the fence, up to the very moment of being frightened by the gardener.

"That is a very interesting story. Wait right here. I'm sure he'll want to see that egg."

That being said, the gardener walked toward the house.

Behind him the boys fought over one last tomato. Nipping and wrestling around on the ground, they failed to notice the door of the house opening.

"Give it to me, you already had three, I only had two."

"So what, I got it and I'm bigger than you."

As they fought over the tomato, it rolled out of their grasp. They both hunched their back legs and prepared to leap for the fruit when the end of a long wooden shaft speared the tomato, crushing it, spraying it's juice over the brothers faces.

"And I'm bigger than both of you," boomed a voice from above them, "Now, knock it off!"

The boys froze in their tracks and slowly looked up. Above them stood Malik, the wizard.

The End, Part 1

2

The Quest

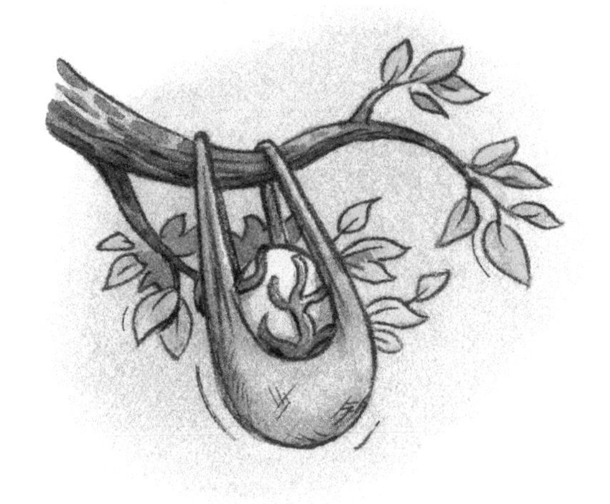

The wizard, Malik, was great in stature, not of height mind you, but of deed. Having spent much of his youth learning from exploring his world; he was now quite content to share that knowledge with the youth of the day. He took much care in working with his potions and reading from dusty old manuscripts; but was equally devoted to tending the herbs in his garden.

Presently in his hand was a hoof spade and at his feet were two young squabbling brothers, Nimby and Orell. Having found a large strange egg and not knowing what to do with it, they'd been advised to come seek his direction; and that he would gladly give. And perhaps, if the brothers were very lucky, they'd learn something about themselves and the world in which they lived.

Nimby and Orell couldn't believe their eyes, "Hey, you're a gardener," chorused the brothers.

"Yes, I am. Does that mean I can't be a wizard too?"

"Um, no. I guess. It just doesn't seem, wizardly, that's all."

"Why don't you take me to this egg you've found and we'll discuss what is wizardly on the way?"

The kids, eager to move led Malik to the egg.

Malik leaned over the egg and pushed his spectacles from the tip of his nose closer to his eyes. "Yes, yes." He murmured, tapping the egg with his walking staff. "Just as I suspected, it's the egg of a Pequid, very hard and nearly sounds ready to hatch."

The kids stepped back and gasped.

Malik smiled, "Nearly ready, this egg won't hatch until it's ready and it won't be ready until it's home."

"What's a Pequid?" asked Orell.

"Where's it's home?" asked Nimby.

Malik pulled out a cloth sling from under his robe and rubbed it against the bark of the tree and into the dirt and grass around the egg. "Wouldn't want to loose your

way back, would you?" he asked with a wink.

The boys looked to each other then back to the wizard.

"Remember these words, keep them close to your hearts. For a wonderful journey, you both shall soon start."

The boys watched and listened as he carefully wrapped the egg in the sling while giving them these instructions on its return...

Keep traveling east from our village, both go
To return the Pequids egg you must go with the flow

Depend on your brother you have what you need
But you must work together if you are to succeed

A fast friend you will find in an unlikely place
To guide you in travel and set the eggs fate

When you enter the forest, make no unnatural sound
Or what you need to get home will be froze on the ground

From earth then water shall come forth what you seek
and return to the forest what it needs to breathe

The scent of the earth and the bark of this tree
Like a beacon to a green flying carpet will be

At that moment Malik slipped his hand into a pouch and tossed some type of powdery herb into the air. The boys watched as the green shimmering powder descended around them and faded away as it neared the ground.

"Wow". The boys turned back to Malik but he was gone, vanished into thin air.

"Wow". The wide-eyed brothers were stunned. He was a wizard all right, a real wizard. The words he spoke made perfect sense, and none at all, and, he could disappear.

The kids rushed home as fast as they could, carrying the egg between them in the sling Malik had provided. They told their mother of the meeting and that they must take the egg to it's home. With their mother's approval, the kids began the first leg of their journey, which was to cross the Babbling Brook.

The kids bounded down the path from their house, each holding opposite ends of the sling, the egg dangling between them. Through the town they went, past the grain shop, the hoofery, (what we'd call a blacksmith), the 'All You Can Graze' outdoor market and then past the last few houses in town.

They continued through a few fields and approached the edge of the brook, which was really more like a stream. The closer they got the louder was the sound of the water as it flowed over and through the stones in its path. The kids stopped a few feet from water and set the egg at their hooves.

"How are we going to cross with the egg?"

"We'll run up to the edge and jump across together just like we jump over the fence."

"I don't know, Nimby, it's a long jump."

"It's not that long. We can do it."

Nimby moved to the waters edge and placed his right fore foot into the water.

A squeaky, bubbly voice called out to him from the water,
"Hey, watch it there," and seemed to float away.

"You're mussing up my mud bank with your hooves."
"Yeah, Don't tread on me."
"Me either."

"Hey, stop pushing."
"I'm not pushing, I'm going with the flow."
The brothers exclaimed, "It's the water, it's talking!"
"True, true." the brook, responded, "I am water.
But water doesn't talk."

"I am a brook.
"Yeah, brooks babble."
"What?"
"What...

"About what?"
"What"?
"Hey, stop it!" Nimby yelled.
"I can't, it's what I do."
"Well, can you tell us if we're on the
right path to the rolling hills?" asked Orell.

"Yes, you are."
"You are?"
"Are what?"
"What?"

"What?"
"What?"
"What?..."

"Orell, we're not getting anywhere just babbling.
We should just make the jump."
Nimby picked up his side of the sling.

"But Nimby, it's too long of a jump. We should trot down stream 'til we find a better place to cross."

Orell picked up his end of the sling and the brothers began tugging in opposite directions. The more they pulled, the more the egg bounced between them. Then the unthinkable happened. The egg flew out of the sling and into the brook.

"Oh no!" cried Orell.

Nimby took a step into the brook but it was too deep.

"What are we going to do?"

"Don't worry," babbled the brook, "I got it.

"No, I got it."

"No, I got it."

"I got it."

"I got it..."

As the egg vanished from sight, a small whirlpool appeared in its midst and the brook spit out the egg which soared high through the air. Nimby grabbed the handles of the sling in his mouth and bounded over the brook and up the bank on the other side with Orell a step behind him. He then released one end of the sling and Orell clenched it and pulled, opening it. As he did the egg fell directly into it.

The brothers continued up to the top of the bank where they stopped and set the egg down.

"Wow, that worked well."

"Why don't we take turns carrying the egg?"

"Okay." answered Orell, "you first."

"Harrumph," grunted Nimby as he picked up his end of the sling and waited while Orell picked up and draped his end of the sling over Nimby's head.

Then he turned and shouted back to the brook, "thank you," and moving closer to his brother, giggled, "and thank you too."

On they went, leaping over rocks, bushes, and dips in the path, all the while the egg dangled from Nimby's neck. They began to hear and feel a low rumbling. It sounded like a long freight train passing through a canyon and it tickled their hoofs.

Leaping over a large fallen tree trunk, they were stunned by what stood before them, the Rolling Hills of Mudhurn.

The kids couldn't believe their eyes. They'd heard of rolling hills, but who would have thought the hills were actually rolling. They looked like great coils on a wiggling rope.

Even Nimby was afraid. Orells legs were shaking, and not from the vibration of the hills.

The brothers huddled close to each other.

"What are we going to do?"

"I don't know, Orell."

"I don't know about this, Nimby. Maybe we could find another way?"

What they didn't realize was that they were already moving. The ground beneath them was slowly moving forward. Orell folded his legs beneath him and tucked his head beneath his breast, shivering.

Nimby braced himself and before he knew it, he was riding the hills.

"Wee." shouted Nimby over the sound of the hills as he flung himself into the air leaping back and forth from hill to hill. "Come on Orell, don't be such a baby."

"I'm not a baby, I'm older than you are!"

"Yeah, by two minutes."

"That's still older than you are," said Orell as he timidly rose up on his legs and took a step. "If I'm a baby, you're a baby."

"Am not!"

"Are too!"

"Baby. Baby. Orell is a baby!"

"I may be a baby, but I'm smarter than you are!"

Orell sat back down in a huff.

"Aww, come on Orell. I was just playing. Come on, Orell, it's fun."

Nimby leapt straight up and when he landed another hill had moved beneath him.

"Can you do that?"

"Orell leapt from his sitting position, hurling himself with such force and grace that he flew like an arrow, passing over Nimby and landing on the next hill in front of them.

"Wow," gasped Nimby.

Not to be outdone, Nimby flung himself forward into the air somersaulting and landing on his feet in the same spot. But as he did the egg flew out of the sling.

"Look," shouted Orell, nodding his head toward the egg.

They both bounded down the hill after the egg as it tumbled and rolled along as fast as they could trying to catch it.

But before they could, it bounced back into the brook, which was at the foot of the hill. Only now, it really was a stream.

As they neared the brook, the egg rose from the water on what looked like a wet plank of wood.

The boys stopped in their tracks.

"Wha..."

As the boys watched, big eyes appeared on both sides of the plank. Then, behind the egg appeared two huge teeth.

"Oh no!" Stammered the brothers...

The End, Part 2

3
The Return

From the very deepest part of the brook came a creature, a creature starved by loneliness, crazed by boredom, and driven mad by the babblings of the brook. Something within the beast had stirred, something it hadn't felt in a long time. Something was coming its way. The vibrations suggested it was round, had weight to it, and was descending fast. The creature swam up to meet it, circled it several times and nibbled at it. It was good. The creature decided it was safe and cradled it in his chest as he made his way to the surface.

Careful not to put itself into danger the creature hid behind the round thing it had found and took a peek out of the water. To its surprise, there were two young Bodusis standing near waters edge.

There was no way the creature could know that what it had discovered was the egg of a Pequid; or that the Bodusis had found the egg, and been challenged by a wizard to return it to it's home. All the creature knew was that this was an opportunity not to be missed.

It slowly raised its brown head from the water behind its prize.

"Oh no, " stammered the brothers, "it's a beaver."

The beaver slowly grinned, revealing two long crooked teeth, separated by a big gap, and began tossing the egg in the air with it's tail.

"Hey," shouted Nimby, "that's our egg."

"Don't think so. No, no. Don't think so," barked the beaver, making a whistling sound when he spoke. "My woody round thing. My woody round thing."

"It's not a woody round thing. It's an egg, and it's ours."

"No, no. Mine. Mine. Woody round thing, woody round thing."

The boys gasped as the head, tail, and egg disappeared beneath the water.

They ran to the edge of the brook but couldn't see a thing.

Finally, further down the brook, the beaver surfaced; this time floating on it's back with the egg on its belly. Its tail paddled from side to side, pushing it around in a small circle.

"Woody round thing, woody round thing."

The beaver sprayed water in the air like a miniature fountain from the gap between its teeth.

Nimby took a few steps back and motioned for Orell to follow.

"That beaver is nuts!"

"Probably so, Nimby. But what do you expect? It does live in a babbling brook."

The kids looked back to the beaver, which was now sitting on a rock in the middle of the brook, tossing the egg in the air with its tail, and catching it in his arms.

"That gives me an idea." Orell, began whispering in Nimby's ear and they moved back to the waters edge.

The beaver was now trying to balance the egg on its head.

"Hi, let me introduce myself. I'm Orell"

"And, I'm Nimby. What's your name?"

"Beaver Beaver. Beaver Beaver."

"Hi Beaver Beaver, where we come from, there's a game that's really fun and everyone plays it. It's called, "Egg Toss"...I mean, "Woody Round Thing Toss." You see we use a sling like the one Nimby's got around his neck."

Nimby pulled off the sling and set it at his feet.

Orell continued, "2 players hold the sling between them and the one with the egg-uh, woody round thing tosses it into the sling. If it goes in, you win."

"Yes, yes. I can do that. I can do that. Woody round thing. Woody round thing."

"Okay." shouted Nimby, "Let's play! Let's play!"

The brothers lifted the sling by holding the handles in their mouths and pulled away from each other making a pouch.

"I can do it, I can do it. Woody round thing, woody round thing."

Beaver Beaver tossed the egg into the air and leapt up after it, catching it mid air with its tail and flung it in a high arch toward the kids.

"I got it," growled Orell through clenched teeth pulling back on the sling.

"No, I got it," growled Nimby, tugging at the sling. Both brothers tugged in opposite directions pulling it tight as the egg sailed straight into it. The egg bounced out of the sling and flew high over their heads and out of sight. The boys listened and thought they heard a faint splash in the distance.

“Woody round thing gone! Woody round thing gone!”

Beaver Beaver barked as it leapt in and out of the water, using it’s tail to slap water all over the boys.

“Hey, stop it,” yelled Nimby.

Beaver Beaver kept up its antics, leaping in and out of the water traveling along with the flow of the brook crying, “Woody round thing gone, woody round thing gone.” It’s voice faded as it to faded in the distance.

Soon, all that was left was the sound of their panting and a whispering wind, which soon hushed them.

“Now what are we going to do,” Orell bleated?

“The egg is gone, it’s all our fault!”

For once Nimby was at a loss for words. He wanted to comfort Orell, but he couldn’t think of anything to say. He felt terrible. Finally he whispered, “I’m sorry Orell. Should we try and follow the stream?”

In the distance they heard voices approaching. They seemed to be getting closer, but they couldn’t make out what they were saying. Slowly the voices became clear.

“I got it. No, I got it. No, I got it, and hey, how many times do we have to tell you? I’m a brook, brooks babble. Streams run.” The kids had completely forgotten the brook could speak and were overjoyed that they weren’t alone.

“You almost caught it. Keep following the sun to the forest and meet me at the center. You can pick up the egg there. That’s where everything I carry ends up.”

“Why can’t you just spit it out, asked Orell?

“I can’t spit it out because it’s already too far away. It’s gone over my fall.

“Well, why can’t we just follow you there,” asked Nimby?

“I go under the ground and become an under ground stream; to bring water to the forest. I come back to the surface in middle of the forest as a pond,” said the voices from the brook. “You have to climb to the top of the bluff and stay on the path. See you there. See you there. See you there...”

The voices trailed off, Nimby scooped up the sling again, and the boys began climbing the bluff. As they reached the top they could see before them a forest of towering trees.

"Remember what the wizard said? We've got to be quiet once we enter.

"I know."

"Extremely quiet."

"I know. I know. Orell, you don't have to keep telling me.

"Well, I just thought...

"Every sound, great or small must be oh, so natural."

"Oh," exclaimed Orell, "You sound so, so..."

"Wizardly? Thank you. But, a lot of what he said, honestly, I don't get at all."

The bothers nuzzled each other both knowing this was to be the hardest part of all. They closed their mouths and trotted into the forest.

Butterflies and ladybugs danced in and out of the sunlight as it streamed though the tops of the swaying trees. Small forest creatures scampered about, nibbling on

shoots of grass and quenching their thirst by licking up drops of dew. Deeper and deeper the path led them into the forest as the trees became more and more dense.

They crawled over and around twisted limbs and roots, wiggling through tangles of roots, never speaking. Their only communication was through grunts, head nods, and glances with their eyes. The further they went, the less light shown through, yet they continued in the dark. Orell followed closely behind Nimby. The shadows frightened him. As Nimby struggled through a dense patch of brush, he became so entangled he couldn't get out.

Orell lowered his head, leapt forward and butted Nimby in the rear pushing with all his might. Bursting free, Nimby yelled, "Ow! That Hurts!"
"Oops."

There was a great deep moan from the forest and the sound of leaves falling to the ground like rain.
Then a ghostly quiet; nothing stirred. Nothing.
Even the wings of a dragonfly perched on a twig were still.

The brothers huddled together not daring to move and barely breathing. They held each other wide eyed, realizing what they had done. They had petrified the forest. Their heads hung to the ground and they moaned in despair. It was their fault. If they hadn't been fighting, the egg would not have been lost, twice. And now the forest was frozen, too.

Just then, the strangest thing happened. The ground began to get wet at their hooves as if the tears from their eyes were making a small puddle. The puzzled kids backed away as the puddle grew and grew, bubbling and churning mud and leaves. A familiar squeaky, bubbly voice asked, "You looking for this?"

From the center of the pond erupted the egg. The trees began to tremble and moan. As the egg rose up on a pedestal of water, Nimby spoke Maliks words,

**From water and earth shall come forth what you seek
and return to the forest what it needs to breathe.**

Like magic the leaves swooped under the egg in the shape of a cup and lifted it into the air. Wave upon wave of leaves swarmed the egg. It seemed as if every leaf in the forest wanted to touch the egg. The egg was lifted higher and higher and began swaying back and forth as the leaves swarmed beneath it.

The kids strained to see the egg as it rose up to the treetops. Then the deep voice of every tree in the forest roared out, "Now!"

The leaves scattered in all directions returning to the branches as the egg plummeted to the earth. With a loud thump, the egg struck the ground and shattered, leaving only the veins on the outside wrapped around a group of tiny leaves.

The kids watched in awe as the veins slowly unfurled and stretched out rooting themselves into the earth. The tiny sprig righted itself and seemed to glow with pride. The baby leaves danced around the sprig in their new found freedom then gently attached themselves to the ends of its tiny limbs.

Pequids were trees!

"Wow," sighed the kids. And just at that moment it seemed as if the very air had turned green. You see, the forest trees were overjoyed at the return of their young and showered the kids with grateful leaves.

The brothers and the leaves began dancing, leaping to and fro. After playing for what seemed like hours, the boys were ready to go home.

But how were they going to get home?

If they were fortunate enough to find their way, it would surely take hours and it would be night.

"Nimby, we're lost. What are we going to do?"

"I know, we'll ask the Babbling Brook."

They looked and sniffed for the pond, but it was gone.

While they were playing, the brook had moved on,
leaving just a muddy footprint. They sat on the forest floor, exhausted.

"We must be missing something, Orell."

"We must. But what?"

Orell looked at his brother, the tattered sling still draped around his neck wondering if he looked as worn out as Nimby did.

Orell eyes widened and he rose up. "I've got it!"

Nimby stood up. "What?"

The scent of the earth and the bark of this tree
Like a beacon to a green flying carpet will be

Orell pulled the sling from Nimby's neck and rubbed it in the leaves. The treetops above them began to sway and the branches and tree trunks creaked and moaned.

"Home," bellowed the trees.

The leaves began to swarm around and underneath them lifting the brothers higher and higher into the air. Soon they were floating toward home on a bed of leaves.

In just a few minutes they had traveled directly above the spot were they'd found the egg and the leaves gently set them down under the big tree in the lot. Then in a huge flock, the leaves flew away in the direction of the forest.

Nimby laid on his back, arms folded behind his head. As he rested on a log, he gazed up at the drifting clouds and sighed, “Wow, that was incredible.”

“It sure was,” answered Orell, as he blew on a dandelion, setting free its blossoms. He watched them float away, and turned to Nimby, “I want to do it again”.

“Me too,” murmured Nimby.

Orell sat down next to Nimby in the warm afternoon sun and they both closed their eyes remembering.

The End

CPSIA information can be obtained
at www.ICGtesting.com
Printed in the USA
LVHW071410210120
644219LV00004B/15